For Jinx, with love—P.G.
For Genny—C.J.C.

Text copyright © 2003 by Pippa Goodhart
Illustrations copyright © 2003 by Caroline Jayne Church

First published in the United Kingdom in 2003 by The Chicken House,
2 Palmer Street, Frome, Somerset, UK BA11 1DS

Reinforced Binding for Library Use

Library of Congress Catologing-in-Publication Data available

ISBN 0-439-45699-1

10 9 8 7 6 5 4 3 2 1   03 04 05 06 07

Printed in Singapore

First American edition, April 2003

Pudgy

A Puppy to Love

by Pippa Goodhart
Illustrated by Caroline Jayne Church

The Chicken House

SCHOLASTIC INC.
New York

Nobody will play with Pudgy . . .

So they are sad . . .

and then Pudgy is bad.

all on his own.

Pudgy licks Lucy . . .

so they play together . . .

and they stay together.

Forever . . . .

and ever.